D0395346

OTHER YEARLING BOOKS YOU WILL ENJOY:

YEARLING BOOKS are designed especially to entertain and enlighten young people. Patricia Reilly Giff, consultant to this series, received her bachelor's degree from Marymount College and a master's degree in history from St. John's University. She holds a Professional Diploma in Reading and a Doctorate of Humane Letters from Hofstra University. She was a teacher and reading consultant for many years, and is the author of numerous books for young readers.

The
PuPPy Sister

S. E. Hinton
Illustrated by Jacqueline Rogers

A Yearling Book

Published by
Bantam Doubleday Dell Books for Young Readers
a division of
Bantam Doubleday Dell Publishing Group, Inc.
1540 Broadway
New York, New York 10036

ISBN: 0-440-41384-2

Reprinted by arrangement with Delacorte Press

Printed in the United States of America

August 1997

10   9   8   7   6   5   4   3   2   1

CWO

To Nick and Aleasha,
my good pups,
and David,
their good dad

One

"**I** didn't say I wanted a dog. I said a brother or sister might have been nice."

That's the first thing I can remember Nick saying.

Nick doesn't remember coming home from the hospital when he was born, but I remember coming home from the farm. That is the first happening I can remember, coming home. And Nick's first words.

"Well, it looks like there's not going to

be a brother or sister, so a puppy will have to do," Mom answered.

I was in my travel kennel, a kind of box with bars at one end, so I could see out. (Nick and I got it out yesterday—I can't believe I could ever fit in that thing!)

Even though I could see out, there wasn't much to see. Just the back of the front seat, but I didn't care because there were too many sounds—cars and trucks rushing by, honking, the engine of our car. And too many smells—gasoline, Nick, Nick's Chee-tos, Mom and Dad, and then bursts of smells as we passed farms and ranches and towns.

I had never been in a car and I was very frightened.

Mom said, "Nick, she's whimpering because she's scared. Pet her a little."

"No way," Nick said. "It'll probably bite me."

"*She,*" Mom said. "Not 'it.' She's a puppy person, not a thing."

I couldn't see Nick because he sat on the other side of the travel kennel. But I could smell him. He wasn't as mad as he sounded.

"Well, okay. But *she* better not bite," he said. His fingers came through the bars and I licked them. They tasted cheesy and very good. His hand smelled so friendly!

"Good girl." Nick's voice was softer. "You're going to be okay."

I felt better.

We stopped and Mom took me out of the kennel and sat me on the ground.

"Here, Nick, take your puppy sister over to that field so she can do her business and stretch her legs."

Nick had a long leash fastened onto my collar so that I couldn't lose him. We ran and ran together. It was so much fun!

Back at the car, Dad poured a cup of water out of a bottle and Nick showed me some food.

But I ignored it. A strange smell from a nearby ditch caught my attention.

I dragged Nick along and peered into the little ditch. I was nose to nose with something! It had very long ears, whiskers, and wild buggy eyes!

The creature's nose twitched. *"Aha!"* He jumped out of the ditch and went leaping across the field.

"Aha!" he shouted in a strange high-pitched cackle.

I didn't hesitate a second. I jumped after him so hard Nick came off his end of the leash.

The creature jumped in zigzag lines. I scrambled fast after him. We were having such fun. What a friendly fellow!

"No, 'Leasha, no!" Nick yelled, chasing

me. "Not toward the highway! Leave the rabbit alone!"

"No, Nick, no!" shouted Mom. "Not toward the highway!"

Mom and Dad joined the chase, too. A chase party!

The rabbit jumped, jumped, jumped. *"Aha!"* he laughed.

I was getting closer, closer—suddenly my head was jerked backward, my legs went out from under me, and I thumped onto the ground.

Nick was stretched out behind me, hanging on to the leash.

He rolled to his feet and grabbed me tight.

"No!" he panted. "Never run into the road."

I could hear his heart pounding. Mom and Dad ran up.

"Nick, never chase that puppy onto a highway!"

I could hear their hearts pounding, too.

What a fun family! They really knew how to do a chase.

Nick rubbed his cheek on my fur. I looked across the highway. The trucks blocked my view for a second. Then I saw a pair of long ears bounding away and heard a faint *"Aha!"*

I whimpered and squirmed but Nick just held me tight.

"Let's hit the road," Dad said.

"We almost did," said Mom.

It was awful to be stuck back in the carrier. I whined. "Oh no you don't," Nick said. "You're not getting out again till we get home."

I remember the rest of the trip being just like that—smells and noises for a long,

long time. Smells and noises . . . the car rocking . . . smells and noises . . . smells and . . .

"Aleasha," Mom said softly. "Aleasha, wake up. We're home."

I woke up to find Mom putting me on the ground.

"Here's your new backyard, Aleasha." I walked around, too tired even to sniff much.

"She needs a good night's sleep," Dad said, "and so do you, Nick. Let's show her the laundry room. That's where she'll sleep until she's housebroken."

They took me into the house and put me in a little room. I had a pillow, a food dish, a bowl of water. I sniffed each. But where were Nick's pillow, dish, bowl?

"Good night, honey," Mom said. She turned off the light and shut the door. It was dark. I was all alone! I started to whimper.

"Here, girl." Mom opened the door and tossed me something. It was an old shirt of Nick's. It smelled familiar already. I took a deep breath of it and closed my eyes.

Then, just before I went to sleep, I caught a new smell. Something different, strange. I couldn't keep my eyes open, but I went to sleep knowing that someone else lived in that house . . .

Someone not human!

Two

My first full day home was very exciting. There were new smells everywhere—most of them with a strong flavor of Nick. I raced around the yard, sniffing.

"Watch, Nick," Mom said. "We're going to see an important meeting."

I was on the trail of something—the same strange smell I had caught the night before. A smell of little dead animals and some kind of weird food, of clean fur and a calm mind . . .

11

I looked up and saw the cutest creature I'd ever seen in my life! I jumped sideways, froze and stared.

She was just my size, a gray ball of soft fur with little white mittens and a white stripe down her throat.

"Oh, run!" I said, unable to move. "Please run."

"Certainly not." She picked up a paw and licked it, then wiped her face. She had very small ears, but she was so cute! I couldn't stand it!

"Can you say *'Aha!'*?" I asked. "Can you say *'Aha!'* and run?"

"Yes." She went on with her cleaning.

"Well?" I couldn't wait to chase her.

"I said I could. I didn't say I would." She gazed at me calmly.

"Come on, run!" I slowly walked up to her, and we touched noses. She had a dry, darling little nose. I sniffed hard, catching her ear. She shook her head. And reached up and tapped me on the nose with her paw.

"Mind your manners, please." Then she went on cleaning her face. For one second she showed me her long curved claws. Then they disappeared.

"I will not run so that you can chase me. I have to do enough of that with strange dogs. I will not be chased by a member of this family."

"Come on," I begged. I poked her with my nose, just to get her started.

"Aleasha! No." Nick's voice sounded so stern that I cringed. "Mom, she's bothering Miss Kitty."

"Honey, they have to get used to each other. They're in the same family now."

I slunk back, ashamed.

"You're part of the family?" I asked.

"Of course," the creature answered.

"You don't look like the rest of us. You sort of look like a rabbit."

"I'm a cat," she said calmly.

"Well, won't I ever get to chase you?"

"No. You may chase Nick. I understand boys and puppies do that sort of thing. By the way . . ." Miss Kitty lifted her head and we touched noses again. "Welcome."

She had a kind face. I yapped sharply. If I could just get her started . . .

"Aleasha!" Mom said. *"No!"*

No! No! No! Boy, did I learn that word those first weeks. Like this:

Nick yelled, "No!" Then, "Mom, 'Leasha's biting me, and she's shoving me with her shoulder!"

Mom said, "She's herding you, like she would a sheep. That's what Australian shepherds do."

Well, of course I was biting him. He

would run and I would chase him and make him go where I wanted. The mystery was—why wasn't he biting me back?

Then he would throw the ball and I would get it and run and he'd start yelling again, "No! Bring it back! Bring it back!"

It was the only way I could get him to chase me. He didn't know how to play at all.

"Nick," Mom would say, "it's time to take Aleasha outside, so she can do her business."

"Just a sec," Nick would answer.

And all of a sudden Mom would yell, "I told you to take her outside! Now you can clean up the mess."

"Oh, yuck!"

"Puppies can't wait just a sec," Mom said.

Nick griped, "If I had a *real* sister I

wouldn't have to do this. Puppies are a lot of trouble."

But then he'd take me outside and we would have fun again.

Dad was the most fun. He always came home just when I was tired, and he'd pull off his shoes and look at the paper. I could lie by his feet and tug on his pants leg, still tired but happy.

Then I'd put my head on his feet and take a deep breath—his feet smelled so strong! It was the best smell in the house.

Everyone always laughed when I did this. I liked it when they laughed. When I ate my food, sometimes my neck seemed too short and my legs seemed too long, so I'd lie down with my legs around the bowl and stick my head in it.

"Come look at Aleasha!" Nick hollered. "She's got her face in the food dish."

Mom and Dad came in and watched. I

decided if this was so cute, I'd do it again. I always got a laugh.

My food was good enough, but what everyone else ate smelled so interesting. Miss Kitty said it was bad manners to whine for food, and they didn't serve table scraps anyway; I'd be sent out of the kitchen if I begged. I listened to her. Miss Kitty was very wise, she said so herself, and always got what she wanted. It was hard to watch her sitting in Mom's lap in the evening, though. It made me so mad I wanted to bite them both.

I learned that if I was quiet during dinner, and kept my eyes open and moved quickly, I could get lots of good-tasting things. Mom sometimes dropped something. Nick spilled. Dad would forget and leave snacks in the living room, on the coffee table where they were easy to sneak.

I was sometimes too fast. I would gulp something before I had time to realize it didn't taste too good. Garlic dip. It can really make you barf.

Nick never did that. If something was strange to him, he very slowly lifted it to his mouth, took just a little nibble, and usually snarled, "Yuck!"

I tried to do that, sniff something strange to eat and push it away. Then I couldn't help gulping it down. But I wanted to do everything like Nick. He did so many fun things!

Like play soccer.

"Dad," Nick yelled, "Aleasha bit the ball and it's ruined!"

And play chase.

"Well, Mom," Nick said, "these pants are torn up, thanks to my puppy sister."

And tug-of-war.

"Oh, great!" Nick looked at his papers. "My teacher said we could *never* say 'The dog ate my homework.' "

All this would be great fun until Nick would get mad and hit at me.

"Mom," he said one day, "Aleasha's annoying me."

He had a bunch of little men on the floor, moving them around, making them talk and hit each other. I certainly didn't see any fun in that.

"I know, honey, but she just wants to play."

"Well, I don't want to play with her right now."

Mom said, "She'll learn as she gets older."

Meanwhile, I was sniffing his little men. They were horrible-smelling. Except for Nick's hand-smell, they didn't smell like anything. An empty, awful smell.

I picked one up. Then I knew why Nick liked them. They were wonderful to chew! My teeth were so itchy all the time, and these were the best! They felt great on my itchy teeth!

It was bliss, until I heard Nick scream, "No! Aleasha!" He was hitting and kicking at me, angry and red in the face! He was so mad he missed, but I cowered anyway.

"Honey, don't, she's just a baby, she didn't know she was chewing up your toys."

"That was a He-man! They don't make those anymore! I don't see why we had to get an old puppy anyway!"

"Nick, it is hard when you get a new family member, and we'll all have to make adjustments. Remember, Aleasha's trying to learn, too. But it'll be worth it, having a puppy sister, you'll see. She'll be your best friend someday."

"Sure," Nick muttered.

"Dad," Nick said one morning, "do I have to go out and get the paper? It's raining."

"You know that's your chore. Besides," Dad said, waving a delicious-smelling thing in the air, "chocolate doughnut."

"I don't know why I have to do all the awfulest jobs," Nick muttered as I followed him to the door. "Just because I'm the kid—"

He stopped suddenly and looked down at me. "I wonder . . ."

Nick taught me a great new game. It was called Get the Paper.

At first, when he tossed the paper, I scooped it up and ran with it. I thought he'd chase me like he did when I ran with his other toys. But Nick just stood on the porch and watched me run. I got puzzled and bored.

"Look, Aleasha." He waved something. "Look what I've got! A puppy yummy."

A yummy! A wonderful, chewy, exciting yummy! I dropped the paper and raced back to him.

"Oh no, Aleasha." Nick put it behind his back. "Where's the paper?"

Finally, that afternoon, we figured it out. I ran and got the paper and Nick traded me a yummy for it.

"Well, that's a good trick," Dad said when we showed them.

"See?" Mom said. "I told you it'd be worth it."

Nick shrugged. "She's okay, some-times."

I was so proud and excited.

Then Nick grinned. "Mom, you'll remember Aleasha's just a baby if I tell you something?"

"Of course."

"Well, she just made an adjustment on your new rug."

"Oh, *Aleasha!*" howled Mom.

Three

"We just got back from the vet's." Mom walked around the kitchen talking to herself, holding one end of a bone-shaped thing to her ear and talking into the other end of it. She did that a lot.

I started nosing my way out of the kitchen.

"Wait till you see her." Mom's voice followed me. "She really is a beautiful puppy. She has a coal-black coat with an ice-white border, and the prettiest little honey-colored details—leg trim and eyebrows and honey-colored eyes to match."

"How was your trip to the vet's?" Miss Kitty asked me.

"It was *scary*," I said. I was sniffing around through the house. Since I had learned what "do your business" meant and to only do it outside, I got to go into more rooms. "But not nearly as bad as you said."

Miss Kitty rubbed herself along the closet door frame. "It's horrible. I hate it! They always put me in a carrier and the vet has three people hold me, and I meow until Mom gets tears in her eyes."

I stopped in the closet and took a deep breath. It smelled so much like Dad! His shoes smelled wonderful. Just like his toes did in the evening when he sat down to read the paper.

It was the best, strongest smell in the house!

"Well, I didn't make Mom cry at the vet's," I said. "I just shook a little, and I wouldn't have been nearly so frightened if all the other animals hadn't left their scared smells."

But I wasn't interested in remembering the vet's. I liked *now.* I looked around the closet. There were a pair of Dad's shoes. My teeth were itchy and I couldn't remember where I'd left my chew toy . . .

I lay down and started nibbling on the heels of Dad's shoes.

"When I think *I'm* going to the vet, I hide under the bed and won't come out." Miss Kitty was a bore sometimes. The heels of Dad's shoes were good and softened up and I started working toward the toes. Suddenly I jumped up.

"What's that?"

There was a strange animal in the room! I couldn't help it, I did a little business on the carpet and let out a bark.

"It's a mirror, silly."

"Do they bite?"

The animal stared straight back at me. I sniffed and sniffed but it didn't have a smell! An animal without a smell! I barked again and it opened its mouth, but no sound came out.

"Aleasha," Miss Kitty said, "that's you."

Then I saw Miss Kitty sitting next to it. What I'd thought was a window was just a picture of the whole closet.

"That can't be me!" I was horrified. "The nose is all wrong! Look at those ears! And I can't be that furry!"

I threw back my head and howled.

"Well, goodness gracious," said Miss

Kitty. "What did you think you looked like? You're quite nice-looking, for a puppy," she added kindly.

"I thought I looked, well, more like Nick, only a girl," I whined. Mom had said I was beautiful, but that, that *thing* looking back at me . . . No wonder Nick got annoyed with me!

"How long have you been in the family?" I asked Miss Kitty suddenly.

"Four years."

"When are you going to start changing?"

Miss Kitty stopped her licking for once. "Changing into what?"

"A people. You know, like Mom and Dad and Nick."

"Change into a human? You must be joking. Why on earth would I want to do that? I'm a cat."

"How about me? Am I going to stay looking like *this*?"

"Only bigger," Miss Kitty said. "You'll change into a dog."

I swiftly made a plan.

"Oh no I won't," I said. "I'm going to change into a person, like Nick. Only a girl. I'm going to grow anyway, so I might as well be a human. Then I'll get to go where he goes and eat at the table, and we can play more things. Why didn't you ever think of that?"

"Excuse me." Miss Kitty arched her back. "I thought I had made myself clear. I am a *cat*." She stuck her tail in the air and stalked off. I didn't pay any attention. I was deciding things.

"Those ears. They'll have to come down. And the nose is going to be a whole lot shorter.

"I'll have to quit running around on all fours like this. And that fur . . ." I frowned.

Fingers. Toes. Elbows. Knees. At least I didn't have much of a tail to get rid of. Talking, that was going to be the hard part. That would take practice. I started practicing.

"Aleasha?" Mom peeped into the closet. "What are you growling at, honey? Oh, the strange puppy in the mirror?"

She picked me up. "It's just you, Aleasha. No need to growl."

Yes, talking was going to take a while.

"I found Aleasha in your closet today," Mom said that evening to Dad. "I'm afraid she had a little accident."

"Oh well, she is still a puppy . . ."

"And I'm afraid your Reeboks are ruined."

"What?" Dad yelped.

"Dad, she's just a baby," Nick said. We were rolling over and over, and I was trying not to bite too hard, and he was trying not to bite too hard, and he was also trying not to squash me.

"Well, you do need new ones," Mom said.

They all laughed. Usually when everyone laughed I'd get so happy I'd throw myself on my back and bounce. But tonight I just thought about my plan, though I couldn't help grinning back at them. Were they in for a surprise!

Fingers. Toes. Elbows. Knees. And talking.

I was about to make the biggest adjustment of all.

Four

"Mom, have you seen how long Aleasha can walk on her hind legs?" Nick asked. "She's really good."

I had made it clear across the kitchen and he gave me a puppy yummy. Nick liked to think he was teaching me tricks.

"That's nice, honey," Mom said. She hadn't seen me at all. "Now find your soccer ball or we'll be late for practice."

"Bye, 'Leasha," Nick said. "I wish you could come, too."

After they left I sat down, growling to myself. I was so mad! Mom didn't notice anything! I could walk clear across the kitchen on my hind legs now. My muzzle was getting shorter, and my ears were coming in a little. I listened to everything everyone said and I could understand almost all the words. And on our walk, a lady had stopped Mom and said, "Why, what an intelligent-looking puppy. The expression on her face is almost human!"

Mom had said, "Oh yes, she's just like a member of the family."

When Mom looked down at me she did stop and give me a funny look for a second. Then she shook her head and we went on.

Talking was *hard*. There was no way I could say "Mom." My lips couldn't move that way yet. When I tried, all that came out was a howl. *"Ooouuu."*

But I was getting close to "Nick." I sat and said "nnkk" to him one day while he watched TV and he made me go outside because he thought I was going to barf.

When Mom heard it she said, "Poor Aleasha. Have you got the hiccups?"

Boy, it made me mad. The way it was going, I'd turn completely human and still be wearing a collar and eating dog food.

Nick was going off to soccer practice, after I'd worked so hard, and I had to stay home. It had to be something fun because they always took a ball with them and Nick always came back smelling like sweat and grass and other kids. I didn't even get to play with that old ball just because the one time I had all the air went out of it.

I stomped around the house. I felt like biting someone. I saw Nick's SEGA game. I grabbed it in my mouth and shook it. It was a stupid thing anyway. All he ever did was punch on it with his thumbs while he stared at the box. Why did he stare at the box anyway? It made some interesting sounds sometimes, once I heard a dog in it, but why stare at it?

I chewed and growled and shook the controls. Nick was having fun and here I was . . .

"Aleasha Ann Davidson!"

I froze. Nick stood in the door. He ran to me and grabbed the controls.

"Bad dog!"

Nick looked very big when he was angry. I was ashamed. I had been bad, chewing one of his favorite things. I stared down at the floor. I felt so guilty! Nick would never forgive me. He would never even play with me again.

"You know what you were doing, don't you? You did it on purpose!" Nick glared

at me. I nodded. I *had* done it on purpose.
I was miserable.

"Aleasha?" Nick's voice changed. "Did
you nod?"

He smelled surprised. I looked at him.

"And—And—" he stammered, "you
won't do this again, will you?"

I shook my head.

Nick tossed his ruined controls away
and knelt down beside me.

"Aleasha, do you understand everything
I'm saying?"

I nodded and jumped into his lap. I
licked his face.

"Wow!" He held my head and looked at
me. "You must be the smartest dog in
. . . wait a sec!"

He turned my head back and forth, staring at me.

"Your ears are different," he said finally.
"And your muzzle's not as long . . ."

I held up my paw.

"That looks like fingers starting to grow. Oh, wow . . ."

Nick sat back and stared. "This is so weird! This is so weird! It almost looks like . . . Aleasha, are you turning into a human?"

He knew! Finally, somebody knew! I was so happy I wanted to flip on my back and kick, but instead I put both paws on his chest, looked him straight in the eye, and grinned.

"Nick," I said, quite clearly. "Nick."

Five

"We've got to keep this a secret right now," Nick told me. We were in his bedroom. He had locked the door and pulled the blanket down over the bottom bunk to make a dark cave.

"I mean, right now, Mom and Dad probably wouldn't believe us. And I don't know what they would do if they did."

"Nick, Nick, Nick, Nick." I was so

proud of my first word I didn't pay much attention to what he was saying.

"Stop saying that."

"No." I surprised myself. Another word! "No, no, no, no, no."

Pretty soon I had a sentence. "No, Nick, no."

Boy, I was getting good!

"Listen to me." Nick grabbed me by the ruff. "You have to pretend to be an ordinary puppy. At least until I find out what Mom and Dad might do."

I tried to say "Yes." It came out "Wes" and I was mad. "Nick, Nick, Nick, Nick, Nick." I had that one down perfect.

"I don't think they'd sell you to the circus or anything, but the way Dad gripes about the car payment sometimes—let's wait to tell them."

I tried "Oooookay." Hey, that was pretty good, too.

Nick sighed. "Aleasha, I have this awful feeling that once you get going you're never going to shut up."

"Mom," Nick said that evening, "you know how you keep saying Aleasha's like a member of the family?"

"Yes."

"Well, what if she really was a member of the family?"

"She really is, honey." Mom smiled.

"For sure? Positive?"

"Nick," Mom said, picking up her newspaper, "Aleasha couldn't be more a member of this family unless she sat at the dinner table with us."

I wanted to yell "Yippee" right then, but I waited until after Nick and I had raced to his room and closed the door.

"Dad," Nick said the next afternoon, "when I took Aleasha for a walk today, a guy tried to buy her."

"He was probably just being nice, teasing."

"No, he said she was just exactly the kind of dog he'd always wanted and asked if I'd take a hundred dollars for her."

Dad looked up from polishing the car. "Haven't I told you about talking to strangers?"

I wondered how Nick would get out of this one. We really hadn't talked to anyone on our walk.

"It wasn't a stranger. It was Mrs. Scott's yard guy. We wouldn't take a hundred dollars for her, would we?"

"No, of course not."

"Not even a thousand?"

"No, not even a thousand."

"Probably not even a million?"

"A million," Dad sighed, "could buy a lot of puppies."

Nick and I froze, horrified.

"But not this puppy," Nick said firmly.

Dad looked down at me and grinned.

"Not this puppy," he agreed.

And one night Nick and I got a scare. We were rolling around, playing tug-of-war with one of Nick's old socks. Mom and Dad were looking at the box when Mom suddenly said, "Aleasha looks different, don't you think?"

"Different from what?" Nick asked.

"Different from the way she used to look."

"She's growing up. She's going to look less like a puppy and more like a dog," said Dad.

"You got that half right," Nick muttered. I giggled and he clamped his hand over my muzzle. "Shhh!"

"I don't know," Mom said. "She doesn't look like the adult Aussies we saw at the farm."

"Probably at that awkward in-between stage," Dad said.

"Probably," Nick said.

Mom was sort of frowning at me. I rolled on my back, let my tongue hang out, and tried to look very puppyish. I felt like an idiot.

"I don't know . . ." Her voice trailed off. I rolled over and lay with my head on Nick's stomach and closed my eyes. He scratched me behind my ears.

We couldn't keep this a secret much longer. I wasn't worried a bit. But Nick was. I could smell it.

Six

"**M**om," Nick announced one afternoon, "I've taught Aleasha some new tricks. Wanta see 'em?"

"Sure, hon," Mom said. She put the groceries down. "I've thought you two must be up to something, spending all that time in your room."

I took a deep breath. This was it!

"Sit," said Nick.

I sat.

"Roll over," Nick said.

I rolled over.

"Shake," Nick said.

I held up a paw.

"That's great," Mom began, but Nick said, "Wait, there's one more."

"Speak," he ordered.

"Fourscore and seven years ago our fathers brought forth on—"

I stopped. Mom smelled so surprised! More than surprised—shocked!

"Aleasha was t-talking?" she stammered.

"Speaking," Nick said. "But she can talk, too. Can't you?"

"Yes," I said.

"Oh," Mom said, and she sat down. There wasn't any chair so she ended up, splat, on the floor. She just stared at us.

"See," Nick said, "she's turning into a human. See how her ears are different?"

Mom picked up one of my ears and rubbed it, dazed.

"Little," I said.

"And her muzzle's not as long. And get how weird her hind legs are—" Nick broke off. Mom's eyes were huge.

"This was all her idea, not mine," he added. "But it's kinda cool, huh?"

"Oh," Mom said. She went to sleep, right there on the floor, very suddenly.

Dad came home early because Nick called him, but Mom's nap was short. She woke up before Dad got home.

"You better get a chair," she said to him, "because you're going to sit down."

Dad looked puzzled, but he got a chair.

"Nick—and Aleasha—have something to tell you." She looked at us. "Go on—both of you—tell him."

We told him.

For a minute I was afraid Dad would take a nap, too.

"But see, even if we won't sell her, we could be rich," Nick said after we had explained. "A talking dog!"

"Are you sure she's changing into a human?" Dad picked me up and stared into my face. I couldn't stop grinning. "Maybe she's just changing into a funny-looking talking dog."

"Aleasha," Mom said, "are you changing into a human?"

I nodded, and Dad sat me down and sighed. "College is going to be more expensive than obedience school," he remarked.

"Can we get her on *The Tonight Show*? Or one of those talk shows?" Nick asked excitedly. "Like 'Puppies Who Turn Human—Fact or Fiction.'"

"Nick," Mom said, "we are not going to get rich unless we win the lottery, and we're not going to be on TV unless you rob a bank. Nobody can know about this but us."

"Can't I even take her to show-and-tell?" Nick whined.

"No, Nick, we're not going to turn her into a freak show or a science experiment. I don't know why this is happening, but I do know that when we brought Aleasha home to live with us, we were taking the responsibility of giving her the happiest life possible, just as we did when we brought you home."

"What happens when she's finished this transformation?" Dad pushed his shoes off. "Where's she supposed to have come from, the cabbage patch?"

"We'll keep her hidden," Mom said

firmly, "until she's through changing. And we'll start telling people we're thinking about adopting. Then, that's where we got her. We adopted."

"Yes. Yes. Yes!"

I rolled over on my back and kicked the air. I was so happy!

"Wasn't this an episode of *Twilight Zone*?" Dad asked Mom.

"This is pretty weird," Nick said, "but you get used to the idea."

Mom said, "Well, weird things happen and people learn to adjust. You know," she added slowly, "we've always been thrilled with you, Nick, but I've thought I was missing something by not having a little girl, too. Red," she said to me, "will definitely be your color."

Dad still looked dazed.

I laid my head on his foot and took a

deep breath. It was wonderful. I sneezed and sneezed. Everyone laughed.

Dad picked me up and hugged me. "A little girl will be great.

"Hey," he said suddenly, "has anyone taken a good look at Miss Kitty lately?"

Seven

Manners! It was bad enough to learn manners when I was a puppy—"No, no, no, Aleasha! Do your business outside. *Outside!*" And now, "No, no, no, Aleasha! Do your business in the potty!"

In the yard, in the potty—I wished they'd make up their minds!

"No begging at the table." I used to hear that all the time. Now it was "Honey, you're going to have to learn to eat vegetables."

"Yeah," Nick said, "you've been nagging for dinner for an hour."

The food that had smelled so good when I couldn't have any didn't taste so good now that I could.

I sniffed at my plate and whined.

"I don't like 'em either," said Nick. "But if you want any dessert you gotta eat 'em. Corn's okay. The yellow stuff."

I looked at my plate. Yellow stuff? It all looked alike. I'd already gulped down my meat.

"Mom, she looks so dorky in that high chair."

"Well, she can't sit at the table yet, she keeps sliding off the chair. She'll outgrow it soon. You have to remember she's still a baby."

"Here." Mom picked up a spoonful of corn and held it up. I couldn't pick up anything yet, my fingers were just beginning to show.

I took a bite and spit it out.

"Oh, gross!" Nick said. "If she gets to do that, so do I."

"Hmm," Mom said. "I need to think about this. Aleasha, your dessert will be one small scoop of vanilla ice cream."

It was *almost* worth vegetables. But not quite.

I loved hamburgers. And hot dogs. They really didn't look anything like dogs and mine wasn't real hot, but what the heck.

My family had thought it was real cute when I lay down and put my face in my dog-food bowl to eat, but when I did that with a plate of spaghetti, it didn't go over too well.

Sometimes, if everything we were having was just too yucky, Mom let me have a bowl of dog food. This was usually at breakfast. Daddy's oatmeal smelled awful. Nick's cereal had too much sugar for a puppy. Mom said it had too much sugar for a *kid*. Mom only drank coffee. By herself. We didn't mess with Mom till she'd had her coffee.

One afternoon I practiced walking around the island in the kitchen. "What dinner?" I asked. My talking wasn't quite perfect. "M's" were impossible, "Mom" still sounded like "Awi," and I still thought there were many more words than anyone needed.

"Snell good." I sniffed hard. But then, it always smelled good, until it was on a plate in front of me.

"Stir-fry chicken," Mom answered. She took something out of the skillet.

"Oops!" She accidentally dropped a piece of chicken on the floor. Quick as a flash, I gulped it down before she could pick it up.

"Now, Aleasha," she started to say. Then she smiled. That afternoon Mom was so clumsy! She must have dropped two pieces of broccoli, three carrots, and a piece of pepper while she was cooking. I caught the pepper before it hit the floor. What was wrong with her?

Later, at dinner, Nick said, "What's the deal? Why doesn't Aleasha have to have any vegetables?"

Mom looked quite pleased with herself. "Aleasha has already had her vegetables."

And, I realized, I had.

"Mom," Nick said one Saturday. Saturday and Sunday Nick had to stay home and watch the TV box. The rest of the week he got to go to school and come home smelling like crayons and baloney sandwiches and lead pencils and lots of other kids. I couldn't wait till I got to go, too! Nick asked, "Can I take 'Leasha for a walk?"

"Yes!" I yelped, jumping up and down. "Yes!"

I always did that when I heard the word "walk." It was one of the first words I'd learned.

"I don't know," Mom said. "It might be dangerous."

"Mom," Nick sighed. "We know enough to make it around the block."

"I mean, dangerous for Aleasha," Mom said. "She still looks like a puppy, but sort of a strange one. She might forget to act like one. She might scare someone."

"Ggrrr," I growled, and showed my teeth. Nick rolled his eyes.

"Yeah, Aleasha, that's really scary. That's

not what Mom meant. Why would a puppy acting like a kid scare somebody, anyway?"

Mom said, "Because it doesn't happen nearly as often as a kid acting like a puppy. This next year is going to be tricky."

"Well, she landed in a pretty tricky family." Nick grinned.

Mom went on, "Be careful. And put on her leash."

"It won't fit Nick," I said.

Mom sighed. "Aleasha belongs in this family, all right."

Nick and I raced up the block.

It was real hard not to nip him and shove him with my shoulder. Dad said it was my herding instinct and Nick said it was my being a bossy girl. But whatever, it took all my self-control just to run alongside him.

"Wait." I slid to a stop, almost jerking Nick to the ground. "Wow!"

There was a great smell!

"Come on, come on." Nick pulled at me. "I'll be glad when you don't have to sniff every bush you see."

A lady came running down the street. Her running was funny, not fast but not slow.

"What doing?" I whispered to Nick.

"Jogging."

"Why?"

"For fun, I think. Or she's afraid she's too fat."

Her face was red and she was panting and it didn't look like fun to me, and she certainly wasn't fat. I was curious.

"Hi, Mrs. Scott," Nick said.

"Oh, what a sweet little dog," she said as she came by. "What kind is it?"

An "it"! How rude!

She stayed in one place, but kept running. Staying in one place but still running! That was interesting. I watched to see how she did it. I tried it, picking up my feet fast, like running, but stayed in place. It was kind of fun. I bounced up and down. Jog. Jog. Jog.

She slowed down.

I slowed down.

She stopped and I stopped.

She stared at me, which was not good manners, but I smiled to show I didn't mind. And stared back.

"What kind is it?" she asked again. Her voice sounded funny.

"An imitation dog," Nick said suddenly.

"Imitation dog?"

"I mean, imitating dog. They do what you do. Kind of a rare breed."

Ouch! Something bit me on the ear. A flea, darn it! Mom said I'd probably have a

few until my fur came off, even though I had to take a bath twice a week.

I reached up and picked the flea off and frowned at it. I crunched it between my thumb and finger. Nasty little bugs! Take that!

Something smelled very startled, and I looked up at the lady. She looked so funny I almost laughed.

"She does tricks, too," Nick said quickly. "That's one of her best. Come."

I trotted off beside him, but when I glanced back at the lady she was standing in the street staring at us, not jogging anymore.

Mom was not happy when she heard about it.

"No more walks for you, young lady. Too risky. Aleasha, you're going to be not quite a human and not quite an animal. It's going to be tougher than you think.

"And pay attention, Nick. It's going to be a little like being a teenager. Changing from a child to an adult is a strange state."

Later I lay at the front door, watching the street. I put my head on my paws. Being human would be tougher than I'd thought. Maybe. But still it would be worth it.

I glanced up and saw the mailman coming down our sidewalk. The mailman! That hat! Those clothes! That bag!

"Hey, you!" I jumped to my feet. "You can't come here! This is my house! Hey, you! Get off my sidewalk!"

He stuck papers in our mailbox like he always did, not even glancing at me. "And don't come back!" I yelled. And then I realized I was barking. Thank goodness!

Eight

"Next year you're going to love Halloween," Nick said. "It is so cool."

He was going through a large sack of mysterious stuff. All the strange smells made me wild.

"Yes!" I rolled on the floor and kicked. "I love Halloween! I want Halloween *now*. I have to have Halloween!"

Actually, I didn't know what Halloween was, but if Nick thought I'd love it next year, I was sure I'd love it now.

"Halloween isn't something you have, Milk-Bone-breath, it's something that happens."

"No name-calling," Mom shouted, but she really wasn't paying attention.

"Why does she talk to that machine? Every time it makes that ringing noise, she ignores us and talks to it."

"She's not talking to the machine." Nick pulled long claws out of the bag. My hair bristled at the sight of them.

"She's talking to Dad. That's a tele-phone. Mom," he called, "let Aleasha say hi to Dad."

I went to the kitchen. Mom held one end of that bone-shaped machine toward me.

"Hi, puppo." Dad's voice came out of the machine! How did he ever get in there? How would he get out?

I scooted backward.

"Barroo," I howled. "Daddy!"

" 'Leasha, 'Leasha, 'Leasha." Nick picked me up. "Silly puppy. Dad's not *in* the phone, he's talking *through* it."

He held me up to the phone, but I wiggled loose and ran.

"She's okay, Dad," Nick said. "I'm telling her about Halloween . . ."

"Halloween is a day, a night, really, when you get dressed up as the scariest thing you can think of."

"You dress up like the mailman?" I asked, shivering.

"Not the mailman," Nick snorted. "Something really scary. Like a ghost, or a monster. See, you get dressed up scary and go around the neighborhood and knock on doors and say, 'Trick or treat,' so they get scared and give you candy so you won't trick 'em."

"But people *like* to see my tricks," I said, puzzled. There sure was a lot to learn, being a kid. Good thing I was smart as a whip, like Dad said. I *still* didn't know what a whip was.

"I'm going to be a werewolf this year," Nick said. He pulled stuff out of his bag. "See, face paint, rubber ears and nose. Fangs. Stick-on fur. You're not going to *believe* how scary I'll look."

He paused, grinning evilly. "I'll look so, so . . ."

"Geeky," Nick said disgustedly, looking in the mirror. "I look really geeky."

His werewolf costume didn't look the way he wanted at all.

I thought he looked scary. Different, anyway. My hair got tingly when I looked at him.

"Put your fangs in," Mom suggested.

70

Nick stuck wax teeth in his mouth. I couldn't help a low growl.

"It's no good." He took them out. "I don't look scary. I don't look like a wolfman. I look like a, a—"

"Puppy," Mom said suddenly. "Aleasha, get up next to him."

We looked in the mirror.

I had changed a lot. My ears were much smaller, the flaps almost gone. My muzzle was shrinking back, my fingers were longer, my arms were shorter in front and longer off my shoulders so that I almost had an elbow. My back legs were straighter, but my knees were still backward. You could see my paws looking more and more like feet every day. It was getting easier to walk upright. Sometimes I could even run. It was a little boring, staying in the house so much, but the changes were so exciting!

"Finally," Mom said, "you look enough alike to be brother and sister!"

We did! It was amazing. Nick's costume turned him into a wolf-puppy.

"I can go Halloween, too!" I yelped excitedly. "I'll look just like a real kid, only made up like a real wolf."

"Werewolf," corrected Nick. "Can she go?" he begged. "Mom, can she?"

"Well," Mom said doubtfully. Nick and I were jumping up and down. "I'll have to ask your dad, since he's the one who always goes with you."

Dad said, "Sure. She looks as scary as Nick does."

He had a normal face, but I could smell him laughing.

"Aleasha's going to have to wear a sweat suit or something," he added. "Nobody would glue on that much fur. And no sniffing people. You'll get arrested."

I was going to have fun! The same kind of fun Nick got to have. Like the fun I would have when I'd changed into a kid and could go to school and camp and soccer practice.

"Now, listen," Mom said as she handed me a paper sack, "people will be giving you candy, but *you can't eat any!* Chocolate is very dangerous to dogs, not that it's great for kids, but you can't eat any candy. All right?"

I was jumping up and down. "I'm going to Halloween! I'm going to Halloween!"

Miss Kitty sat on the arm of the couch. "You're starting to drool."

"What?" I asked.

"You look like a fool."

I stopped and stared at her for a second. "I can't hear you very well."

"Well," she said, "*my* voice isn't changing. Perhaps it's someone's ears."

I was puzzled for a second, then forgot about it as Nick and I ran out the door.

At first it was scary. I had never been out of the house in the dark. When Nick ran up to the first house, I was too shy and I stayed on the curb with Dad. I heard Nick yell, "Trick or treat!" and then, "Thank you!" He ran back to us.

"Come on, Aleasha, get with it. It's not hard."

Boy, his candy smelled wonderful! I went up to the next house with him. I got to ring the bell. A man came to the door.

"Trick or treat!" Nick said. He held out his sack. I forgot what I was supposed to say, but I held out my sack, too.

"Well, well," the man said. "A veritable pack of werewolves! An absolute litter."

He dropped a couple of pieces of candy in each of our sacks.

"Thank you," I managed to whisper.

After that I wasn't scared anymore. I got the idea! *We* were the scary ones. Some people who came to the door actually shrieked at the sight of us.

But a funny thing, none of them *smelled* scared. It was a little hard to smell anything but chocolate, though.

"This next house is so *cool*," Nick said. "They always have the best decorations and the best candy and a spook house set up inside."

"You can't go in this year," Dad said. "I don't want Mrs. Scott getting a close look at Aleasha."

"That's okay," Nick said. Then he whispered to me, "*Sometimes* it's too scary."

It was a big house set in a big yard. When we came up the side walk, I felt my fur start to bristle up. It tickled the back of my neck and fluffed out my sweat suit. I probably looked like the fattest werewolf ever.

"Nick!" I grabbed his hand. "Look!"

"Ouch," Nick said. "Watch the nails, sis. That's just a scarecrow, dummy. They put him out every year."

It was an awful-looking man-thing lying back on a bale of hay.

"What's a scarecrow?"

"They scare crows out of cornfields. It's not a real person. Come on."

I felt a little growl starting deep in my throat. Nick was wrong! That *was* a real *something*. I could smell it. Crows were right to be scared!

I was trying not to whimper when Nick rang the doorbell.

"Ha, ha, ha!" The scarecrow jumped to its feet, laughing a horrible laugh and waving a horrible broom.

"Eeekk!" Nick screamed and jumped off the porch and disappeared into the night.

"Barrooooo!" I howled. I dropped to all fours and barked furiously. *"Barrooo!"* It sounded like a cross between howling and screaming. I scrambled off the porch and raced back to Nick and Dad.

Dad was laughing, but I could still hear the people back at the scary house.

"Now, Jim, that was mean." And someone said, laughing, "Did you see that little girl? I guess she was trying to sound like a wolf. And it sounded exactly like a scared puppy!"

I growled at the house. I wanted to go back there and bite those people!

Suddenly I shivered. "Daddy, I'm cold. I wet my trousers."

"Yeah," Nick said. "Let's go home. I wet mine, too."

* * *

"Oh, oh, oh, oh, oh," I moaned.

I felt horrible! My stomach ached and I felt dizzy.

"Aleasha, honey, what's the matter?" Mom turned on the light.

The light made me even sicker. I tried to sit up in Nick's bottom bunk, then fell back down.

"I'm sick," I whimpered. My stomach bounced and I barfed all over the bed.

"What's wrong?" Nick sat up sleepily.

"Nick, did you sneak Aleasha some candy?" Mom asked.

"Just a couple of pieces," Nick said. "She just kept begging, and some of it *was* hers . . ."

"It smelled so good." I groaned. "I just had to have some . . ."

"Nick, didn't I tell you that chocolate is bad for dogs?"

"You say it's bad for kids, too." Nick

started to cry. "But I don't get this sick."

"It's *poison* for dogs." Mom picked me up and held me.

"I keep forgetting she's a dog," Nick wailed. "You keep saying she's my sister. I'm mixed up!"

"Don't cry, honey, I know you didn't mean to make her sick. But next time listen to me. Go get your dad."

"Vet," Dad said.

"Pediatrician," Mom said.

She still held me on her lap.

"Look," Dad said, "we might still pass her off as a weird-looking puppy, but nobody's going to believe she's just a hairy child."

"Oh," I said, "I feel awful."

"A weird dog who talks?" Mom rocked me. "If Nick were sick we wouldn't call a vet."

"She's so sick because she's still a puppy. She needs a vet."

"Dr. Steven," Mom said. "We'll call him."

"Who's Dr. Steven?" Nick asked.

"He's an old friend of Dad's, a retired pediatrician. He'll help us out."

Dr. Steven came over and gave me some medicine. He did have a funny look on his face when he first saw me. But he was a nice man and so calm you could tell he'd just nod and say, "Umhum," if you told him the house was on fire.

"Have you ever heard of anything like this happening before?" Dad asked finally. He had been waiting for Dr. Steven to be shocked.

"Getting sick from too much candy? Happens all the time."

"No, I mean, a puppy, you know, changing into a, a . . ."

"Sister," said Nick.

"Well, usually a dog stays a dog while becoming a member of the family. Actually, there have been rumors of this happening before, but I've always thought they were tall tales. No real record. Of course, there won't be any real record of this one either." Dr. Steven paused. "Puppy or child, when you bring one home you've taken on a real responsibility. This one is just more . . . ummm, interesting. She had her shots?"

"Rabies, distemper . . ."

"No, I mean diphtheria, tetanus, whooping cough."

"No, I didn't even think of that," Mom said.

"Well, I'll bring them over tomorrow."

Dr. Steven packed up his bag. "And you, young lady, leave candy alone, right?"

"Okay." I nodded. I still felt miserable.

"But really, Steve," Dad said, "don't you think this is sort of *amazing*?"

"The way you normally get kids is pretty amazing, too, if you think about it. See you tomorrow."

When he and Mom and Dad left I asked Nick, "What is the way you normally get kids?"

"Believe me, 'Leasha, you don't want to know."

Nine

It seemed like things changed slowly. For a long time I couldn't figure out why Nick liked to watch TV. I mean, the sound was interesting, I learned about language, but there was nothing on the screen except little moving black dots.

Then one day Nick and I were rolling around on the floor. The TV was on. I was chewing his sleeve, even though I knew better, when suddenly I sat up and barked, "What's that?"

All the dots had formed a picture, a picture of something so awful, so scary, so . . .

"It's Looney Tunes, doofus. Cartoons."

"But they're *weird*."

"They're supposed to be."

I watched a little. Now I could see the pictures on the screen that went with the noise coming out. But it wasn't very interesting. "Let's play catch."

"No," Nick said. "I want to watch this!"

"Nick," Mom called, "would you go see who rang the doorbell? If it's kids with raffle tickets, we'll buy one."

"Let Aleasha do it," he yelled back. "She doesn't want to watch this show anyway."

"Nick-o-las! You know better."

"I know I have to do everything while the Puppy Princess gets to sit on her fluffy duffy," Nick growled, getting up.

I rolled on my back and bared my teeth in a big smile as he walked by.

"Ha!"

"Oh, hello, Nicky, I've come to see your mother about the charity bazaar. Is she here?"

Ready or not, here came Mrs. Scott!

I rolled over and scrambled behind the couch. There was nowhere else for me to hide.

"Mom!" Nick hollered. "Mom."

He trailed Mrs. Scott into the TV room. I didn't like the way she smelled, like globs and globs of flowers.

"By the way," she said, "whatever happened to that interesting puppy you had? The imitation dog?"

"Imitation dog?" Mom asked as she came into the room.

"I guess I mean 'imitating dog.' You know, it did such interesting tricks."

"It"! I stifled a growl as Nick said, " 'It' sure did."

"Oh, we had to give her away," Mom said. "Nick was allergic."

"I sure am," Nick said. "I mean, was."

"But Nick enjoyed having a companion, and his dad and I loved her, too, so now we're thinking of adopting."

"Well, that is exciting, Nicky."

"Thrilling," Nick said. Every time Mrs. Scott said "Nicky," I could smell him snarling.

"I won't have my things ready until Friday." Mom was trying to herd Mrs. Scott to the front door. "But I'll be over bright and early."

They left the room and I crept out of my hiding place. The front door slammed.

"Do some interesting tricks, 'It,' " Nick said with a sneer.

"Nicky, Nicky, Nicky," I snapped back. He ignored me and watched TV.

"Mom," I howled, "Nick won't play with me!"

"Mom," Nick shouted, "make her leave me alone!"

I reached over and turned the TV off.

Nick jumped up. "You're going to get it!"

He jumped on me and we rolled over and over.

"No biting!" he yelled.

"Says who?" I snapped.

Suddenly I felt a sharp pain. "No biting!" I yelled.

Then Mom yanked us apart. "You two are driving me crazy!"

She swatted Nick with a rolled-up newspaper.

"No TV for you today, young lady!" she said to me.

Nick and I looked at each other amazed. Mom went back to the kitchen. Nick and I were *very* good the rest of the day.

"I've got us out of Thanksgiving," Dad said one evening. "I told Aunt Jan we've all got the flu."

"What's Thanksgiving? What's flu? Is it like fleas?" I asked. I was lying on the floor, looking at a book. Sometimes Mom would look at a book for hours. I couldn't figure out what she was looking at, since hers didn't have pictures.

Mine had pictures. It had pictures of someone animal-ly, but not a dog, wearing clothes, but it wasn't a person. Nick said it was a Little Critter and I looked just like it, but he was teasing.

"Flu makes you sick," Nick said.

"Oh. Like candy."

"Forget it, fuzz-face." He turned to

Mom. "You mean I don't get Thanksgiving dinner?"

"I'll make dinner just for us this year."

"I did mention we're thinking about adopting," Dad said, "and that Nick was allergic to the puppy so we gave her away." He pulled off his shoes, like he did every evening, to read the paper.

"What?" Give me away? I put my paws —no, hands—on his knees.

"Aleasha, we have to explain where you the little girl came from. Adoption can take a long time. And we have to explain where you the puppy disappeared to. This is just a little complicated, you know."

"Oh." I went back to my book. Complicated was for grown-ups.

"What's the matter, honey?" Dad asked. "You're frowning."

"Daddy," I said. I sat up and rubbed my nose. "Your feet—they *stink*."

Nick almost fell off the couch laughing. Dad sighed. "I guess that's a good sign."

"Progress," said Mom.

"What's that?" I sat up and stared at the TV.

"The Nutcracker," Mom said. "These holiday specials start earlier and earlier."

"Yuck," Nick said as he flipped channels.

"No, no, no, no, *no.*" I jumped up and down. "Put it back."

He did. "But what are they *doing*?" I asked.

"Oh, they're dancing. That's called ballet."

"I want to do that!" I stood on my toes. I twirled around. I jumped up in the air. "Oh, I *could* do that!"

Miss Kitty was watching me. "You look like a fool."

Was that what she'd said?

You're starting to drool?

You dance like a mule? What had she said?

"What?" I stopped and watched her take one paw and clean her face. It was so cute! But what had she said?

"I can't understand Miss Kitty anymore."

"I never could in the first place," said Nick.

I was puzzled, and a little scared. Would I never know what she was saying again?

Later that evening Miss Kitty came and got into my lap for the first time. I stroked her head. I didn't want to chase her at all.

She half-closed her eyes and started to purr.

I understood.

Ten

"You're going to love Christmas," Nick said. Mom and Dad had brought a *tree* inside, and everybody helped hang little things on it and put up lights and set little figures around the house. Santas, angels, cookies, what did it all mean? I was getting tired of so many things to understand.

"Lots of presents," said Nick on Christmas Eve.

"Peace on earth, goodwill toward men, women, and dogs," said Dad.

"Birth of Christ, God's present to us," said Mom.

"Okay," I said. The cookies smelled good, but I didn't want to eat one. Nothing tasted right anymore. The tree was pretty, but not beautiful. I sort of knew what presents were, but I really didn't want anything.

I curled up on the bottom bunk early. Nick was still sniffing around his presents and shaking them.

"What's the matter, honey?" Mom sat down beside me and patted me on the head.

"I don't know, I'm just so . . ." I blurted it out. "It hurts to walk upright all day, but I can't be on all fours anymore. My back hurts. My smells are mixed up. People food doesn't taste right, but the dog food tastes awful. I'm just tired," I whispered. "I don't look like a dog, and not much like a kid . . ."

"I know, honey." Mom patted me. "I know just how you feel. I was so excited when I first knew I was going to have Nick—excited, and a little scared, too, because I knew my life was going to be so different. But it took *sooo* long and my body changed and I couldn't get comfortable, couldn't wear my usual clothes, my back hurt and my ankles puffed out. It was like being on a train there was no getting off of, but look, now we've got Nick. He was worth the train ride. You were a very brave pup to get on this train, but it'll be worth the trip."

I wanted to lick her hand, but I just held it instead. She must have stayed with me until I went to sleep.

* * *

" 'Leasha, wake up," Nick whispered. He shook my shoulder. "It's Christmas, come on, let's go get our presents!"

I opened my eyes and Nick looked so different! I jumped up and looked around the room.

"Aaahhaeeekkk!" I screamed. I ran to the window and looked out. It was *amazing*! I screamed again, running in circles, stopping to look, then running again.

"Mom, Dad!" Nick shouted. "Aleasha's gone nuts!"

"Oh," I gasped. "Oh, what is it? What is it?"

Everything looked so different! And *wonderful*!

"Has she had all her rabies shots?" Nick asked.

"Aleasha, honey, what's wrong?" Mom grabbed me worriedly.

"Everything is so different!" I jumped up and down.

"Different?"

"Yes, everything has a different . . . like a smell!" I said. "Only smells for the eyes! Only smells for the eyes! Everything has a different smell for the eyes!"

Mom suddenly picked up Nick's blanket and a sweatshirt.

"Are these alike?"

"Yes, yes, yes! Beautiful! Beautiful!"

It was like I'd never known what that word meant before. Everything looked so different!

"Colors," Mom said. "Aleasha can see colors. This," she said to me, "is blue." She sat down.

"Mom, are you crying?"

"I'm just happy Aleasha can see colors."

We all looked at Mom. And although I

was still excited, I tried to tone it down a little. If she got any happier, I'd be miserable.

"Here, Aleasha, we all got so excited this morning we forgot about your presents."

I had finally stopped rushing from window to window, and sat staring at the lights and colors of the tree. No wonder they thought it was beautiful! It was!

I tore into the present eagerly. Shoes. Funny-looking, funny-toed shoes.

"Ballet shoes," said Dad. "As soon as you can, you can have lessons."

I jumped up and twirled around. "I'll dance all day. This color?" I touched my shoes. Frosty and light and silky.

"Pink," Mom said. She handed me another package. "Here, I never played with these, but all my friends' little girls like them."

A girl. Sort of. Not a baby, not a grown-up, light hair and a goofy, empty face.

"What can I do with it?" I asked.

"Change its clothes, I guess."

I looked at it for a while. It had that same empty, nothing smell that Nick's figures had under the smell of Nick's hands.

I remembered something. I tested the doll's toes with my teeth.

Ummm. Perfect. It almost made my teeth itch again.

I chewed it up slowly, happily, being careful not to swallow the pieces. Mom didn't mind at all.

The weather got warmer. The days got longer. And I got itchy! I wiggled inside my clothes. I squirmed around at the dinner table. At night I fell out of bed, scratching in my sleep. Mom brushed me and brushed me, while we watched *Sesame Street*, while I learned my letters.

And my fur came out in handfuls.

"You look like a skinned rabbit," said Nick.

My hair was black. My eyes stayed gold brown like they always had been. My skin was so white! Pink right after my fur came out, then just white.

"You're going to need sunblock, young lady," Dad said.

I spent a lot of time in front of the mirror that spring. Who was this?

I was a girl. A real human girl. I could go to school, start ballet lessons, play in the front yard, go to the grocery store with Mom, go to the park with Nick, go to the ball games with Dad. The ball games! My first ball game!

"The best part is the food," Nick said. "Peanuts, popcorn, Cracker Jack," he sang. "I don't care if we never come back."

"Aleasha, better go easy on the junk," Dad said. "You know how your stomach is."

"I've never puked in my life," Nick bragged. I didn't even snarl at him because I was too busy holding Dad's hand. There sure were a lot of people at a ball game!

"Sometimes they hit foul balls over here," Nick said as we sat down. "But the big guys always get them."

The game was so pretty! All the players moved around like ballet dancers. The grass was green, green, green! The lights and the smells and the music and the man who kept telling us what we were seeing; everything was wonderful! And the sky got darker and bluer. I could barely sit still while they threw the ball to each other.

"I want to play!" I finally had to jump up and down. "Can I? Can I?"

"Not this game," Dad said. "But maybe we can sign you up for a league."

Just then the batter hit the ball hard, but it went the wrong way, up and back, and it was coming toward us. Everyone rushed to catch it.

"Aleasha, come back here!" Dad called.

"I'll get it! I'll get it!" I scrambled over benches, leaped over the big kids standing to catch it, jumped straight up . . .

"Did that kid catch that ball with her *teeth*?" someone was saying. "Did you see that jump? She caught it with her *teeth*!"

I barely noticed all the people staring at me. Dad picked me up.

"Are you all right? Let me see your teeth."

I bared my fangs. They stung a little, but I had the ball, white and a little dirty.

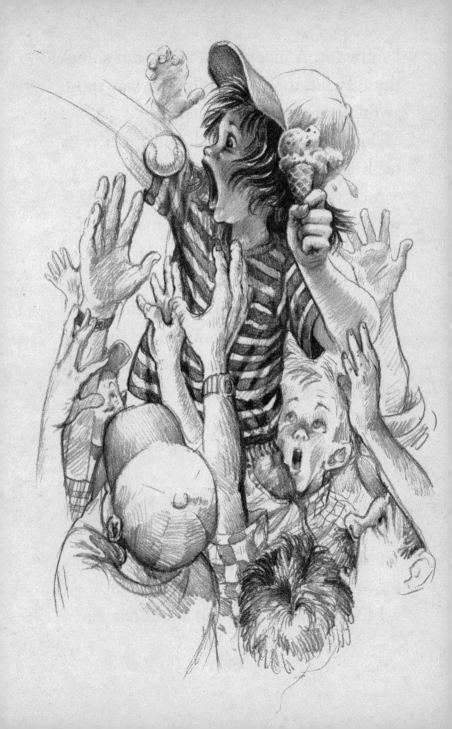

I sniffed it. A nice person smell, but something awful, too. Sort of like the way those awful cigarette things smelled.

"Honey, you can't catch balls with your teeth anymore."

A crowd gathered around us. "Caught it with her teeth! I swear!" someone said. "And you should have seen that jump!"

"Time to go home," Dad said.

We marched right through them.

"Aw, Dad, we just got here! I haven't even got my cotton candy yet," Nick griped. "Aleasha, you're ruining everything."

Dad carried me and Nick trudged behind.

I didn't want to watch ball, I wanted to play ball.

I didn't want to play SEGA and just move my thumbs.

I looked like a girl, but I still felt like a

puppy. It was almost as bad as being a puppy and feeling like a girl.

I put my head down on Dad's shoulder and sighed. "Am I about through changing?"

"No," Dad said. "No one's ever through changing."

I sighed again. Life was hard.

Eleven

"**I**'m *not* trying on any more clothes!" Nick announced. "And I'm sick of standing around the dressing room while Aleasha does."

"Well, I love trying on clothes!" I said. Mom was loaded down with shirts, jeans, and swimsuits, mostly for me.

Mom was right. Red was definitely my color. Blue was definitely Nick's, but he liked purple better.

Mom said, "Let's go eat."

We sat in the food court of the mall. Full of smells! Pizza and hot dogs, Chinese food, hamburgers, cookies! I had a hard time sitting still. A new smell would hit me and I'd twist around, trying to see what it was.

"Can we go home now?" Nick asked.

"We need to get Aleasha a few more camp clothes."

"Aleasha, Aleasha, Aleasha!" Nick griped. "Everything is for Aleasha these days."

Before Mom could answer, a lady stopped by our table. Uh-oh. Heavy flower smell.

"Hello, Susan," she said to Mom. She kept staring at me. "Hi, Nicky, who is this?"

It was Mrs. Scott. I squirmed around. She stared at me so hard. Why didn't she have any manners?

"This is Aleasha," Mom said proudly. "Our new little girl."

"What a bright-eyed little thing!"

I gave her a big, faky grin. Then I cringed and clapped my paw over my mouth.

I was imitating her again.

Boy, was she staring now!

"How old are you, honey?" she asked.

I froze. What was I supposed to say?

"It's about one," Nick said. Nick had blue eyes, like the night sky with stars out, but you couldn't tell when they were this narrow.

"The adoption took a year to complete. She's about Nick's age," Mom said. "But it already seems like she's been with us most of her life."

Mom gave Nick a you're-about-to-be-in-trouble look.

"Well, Aleasha, where do you come

from?" Mrs. Scott asked me. Her hair was red. But not a real red.

"Home," I said. I wished I was there, too.

"Australia," Nick said.

"What?"

"Her biological parents were Australian," Mom put in.

"Shepherds," Nick said. "Australian shepherds."

Mrs. Scott looked very surprised.

"Sheep ranchers," Mom explained. "The actual adoption took place in Texas. It's a long and complicated story, but the important thing is she's part of the family now." Mom got up. "Come on, kids, let's go."

We weren't finished shopping, but I wanted to go. There was something scary in Nick's voice. Was he trying to make trouble?

"Well," Mom said when we were in the car. "What was *that* all about, mister?"

"I don't care!" Nick burst out. "Aleasha, Aleasha, Aleasha! Everything is for Aleasha! I don't know why I have to have a sister anyway! I just wanted a dog!"

"Liar! You said you didn't want a puppy!" I couldn't growl because my throat was too tight. "On the way home from the farm you said you wanted a sister."

"Whatever," Nick muttered. "Everything was fine before."

Nick didn't want me? I looked at him and he was scowling. I tried to smell his feelings, but my nose was all stuffy and my throat choked me. All of a sudden there was water pouring down my face.

"What is it?" I choked. "What's happening?"

"You're crying, honey, because your

brother is being mean to you. I wish I could say this will be the only time, but it won't be."

"I'm sorry, Aleasha, I didn't mean it." Nick put his arm around me and patted me. "Don't cry."

I looked up. "This is crying?" I sobbed. "Oh, wonderful!" Nick stared at me.

"Hey," Nick said, "crying's not wonderful."

"Yes it is," I wailed. In a strange way, it felt good.

"It's not."

"It is."

And finally Mom yelled, "Stop it!" so we did.

That evening Dad said, "Come here, you two."

Nick and I quit playing keep-away and rolled to Dad's feet and sat up.

"I heard you had a fight this afternoon."

Nick and I looked at each other. For a minute we couldn't remember what he meant.

"I just want to tell you—you're going to have fights like that, but never drag them out, or make them last."

I remembered now. But why would anyone want being miserable to last longer than it had to?

"Always stay friends. That way, after we're gone, you'll have someone to share your childhood memories."

"Dad," Nick protested. "She's already important to me. We're not going to have fights."

"Yes you are," Dad said. "And sometimes they're fun to remember. Once your aunt Jan bit me in the back, and when I ran to show Nana, Jan said I did it myself. Just always let it end."

"Daddy," I said, puzzled. "You said we

would share memories after you're gone. Where're you going?"

Mom looked up from her newspaper.

"Hawaii."

"I'd say she spent her first year in dog years, so she's approximately a seven-year-old human. And I think I can almost guarantee she'll spend the rest of her life as a human."

Dr. Steven was giving me a checkup. I had to get some new shots, too, but that was over and I had put my clothes back on. He had gray eyes that matched his hair. It looked nice.

"Well, she is an exceptionally attractive little girl," Mom said proudly. "With her black hair and honey-colored eyes."

"Well, her teeth will probably always be just a little too sharp . . ."

I grinned at him.

"And her ears just slightly too pointed . . ."

I pulled my hair back and grinned some more.

"It gives her a pixie look," said Mom.

"And most people would glance twice at her toes . . ."

"They're exceptionally strong toes," said Mom. "She's great at ballet, and you should see her herd a soccer ball."

"And she'll probably always have an affectionate and enthusiastic personality—"

"Yes!" I jumped up and hugged Mom around the neck. "I will always be affectionate and enthusiastic." I paused for a second. "Whatever that is."

"Other than that, I'd say she is a perfectly normal little girl," finished Dr. Steven. "But do watch out for chocolate."

"Tell me, Steve, really," Mom said just as we were ready to leave. "Have you ever heard of anything like this happening before now?"

"Well." Dr. Steven scratched his head. "As I said, there have been rumors, which I always dismissed as a doctor's version of an urban legend."

"What's an urban legend?" I asked.

"A story that passes for truth, but it's not," Mom answered. "Go on, Doctor."

"Something like this supposedly took place about a hundred years ago, and one just after World War Two—a puppy gradually changing into a human. Of course, nobody could verify these stories. Maybe the families kept quiet. The strange thing is . . ." He paused. We waited. "The strange thing is, both cases were reported as happening in Australia."

* * *

Nick and I were up in the fort, playing X-Men. Nick was a supermutant wolverine hero.

"You'll be Mutant Girl, my faithful sidekick," Nick said.

"No," I said. "I'll be your faithful sidekick, Aleasha Ann Davidson."

"Aleasha! You said you'd play X-Men with me if I played ball with you."

"I will. But I'll be supersidekick Aleasha Ann Davidson. I worked hard to be her, I don't want to be anyone else."

"Okay." Nick gave in. He handed me a sword and we battled villains off the fort for a while. Nick was still fighting, making sword noises, when I stopped and looked at our house.

It was almost dark. Through the patio doors I could see Mom in the kitchen, chopping things. She dropped something, looked down for a minute, then picked it up and threw it away. Dad was on the couch, watching the news. His sock had a hole and his toe stuck out. The lights in the house looked golden against the coming nighttime.

I had such a glad feeling. I jumped up and down. "Oh, Nick, our house . . ." Looks? Smells? Feels? ". . . Our house is so happy!"

Nick stopped his battle and looked at the house.

"You're nuts, Aleasha."

"It is, it is!" I threw my arms around Nick and we fell off the fort into a pile of leaves.

"I love you, brother!"

"Yuck!" Nick pushed me off. He wiped his face with his sleeve. "I *hate* kisses!"

We stood up. He was scowling, but I have a secret I haven't told even Mom. I can still smell love.

I put one hand on each side of his face and looked him straight in the eyes.

"I promise. No more kisses."

Then I leaned over and gave him a big, sloppy, wet lick on the nose.